Praise for

SOMETHING BEGINNING WITH P

'The poems are written for children, which suits all of us. Buy it for your favourite niece. Keep it for yourself.' OLIVIA O'LEARY

'A dream for parents hoping to inspire a love of poetry, and a book that will never be outgrown.'
IRISH INDEPENDENT

'Is álainn an leabhar é agus beidh sult le baint as go ceann na mblianta.' *LÁ*

'Top-class illustration and design complete a must-have package for every school, library and home.' *TODAY WITH PAT KENNY*

'The most marvellously produced piece of work I have seen in a long time. An investment – a brilliant book.' ROBERT DUNBAR

'If some word-gobbling wizard came and snatched all the poems out of this anthology, it would still be a pleasure to browse through. Every page is a dramatic, often zany display of characters, creatures and tumbling objects, all in spectacular colours.'

GORDON SNELL, *THE IRISH TIMES*

SEAMUS CASHMAN founded Wolfhound Press (1974–2001) as a literary and cultural publishing house that achieved an international reputation and many book awards. A former teacher and editor, his own books include two co-edited volumes, *Irish Poems for Young People* and *Proverbs & Sayings of Ireland*, and his poetry: *Carnival, Clowns & Acrobats*, *That morning will come*, *The Sistine Gaze* and forthcoming *Talking down the clock.* He is a creative writing and poetry workshop tutor.

POETRY IRELAND is the national organisation for poetry in Ireland. It is committed to creating performance and publication opportunities for poets and ensuring that the best work is made available to the widest possible audience. www.poetryireland.ie

THE O'BRIEN PRESS has been publishing since 1974, with a particular focus on children's books. The Press is recognised internationally for its significant contribution to children's literature, and it has a long list of fiction in translation worldwide. www.obrien.ie

This revised edition first published 2020 by The O'Brien Press Ltd, 12 Terenure Road East, Rathgar, Dublin 6, D06 HD27, Ireland.
Tel: +353 1 4923333; Fax: +353 1 4922777. E-mail: books@obrien.ie; Website: www.obrien.ie
Originally published as part of *Something Beginning with P: New Poems from Irish Poets* (2004).
The O'Brien Press is a member of Publishing Ireland.

ISBN: 978-1-78849-178-5

Editor's Acknowledgements: For assistance with translation, many thanks to Diarmuid Ó Cathasaigh and the individual poets. To all the poets and illustrators who are represented in this volume, my sincere thanks and appreciation. To The O'Brien Press, who had the idea for *Something Beginning with P* all those years ago; to Poetry Ireland, who endorsed and supported it; and to the Arts Councils, north and south, my sincere thanks.

7 6 5 4 3 2 1
24 23 22 21 20

Printed by L&C Printing Group, Poland.
The paper in this book is produced using pulp from managed forests.

The O'Brien Press received assistance for *Something Beginning with P: New Poems from Irish Poets* from

Published in

DUBLIN
UNESCO
City of Literature

LOTTERY FUNDED

POEMS FROM IRISH POETS

Edited by Seamus Cashman

Illustrated by Corinna Askin and Alan Clarke

Typographical illustrations by Emma Byrne

THE O'BRIEN PRESS
DUBLIN

CONTENTS

EDITOR'S INTRODUCTION
WORDS ON FIRE

Yes, Reader Friends and Strangers, *Words on Fire!* What a great metaphor! Take a moment, sit back and close your eyes. Now see a poem you remember and watch its words scroll across your mind, imagine them coming alight, going on fire, lively flames swirling from word to word as each passes by, creating bright flickering excitements.

You are just imagining. But poems bring words to life (like the phoenix in mythology). Poems awaken words; fill words with fires of energy, beauty, adventure, love, and wonder; and, too, of possibilities your own mind might invent. These words can bring you, the reader, with them on their wings of fire.

That's what poems are — new things to experience. That's what they do for you – awaken, surprise, excite, and comfort you; impel you into action; enwrap you in something different; and often, too, reveal you to you! That's what poets know poems do in lines and verses made of words on fire.

Poems have been around since humans could communicate in words; perhaps even before that, when people used signs, gestures, and unformed words to express themselves (like our emojis today!) We don't have writing from the 'first man and first woman' era. But we do have poems from long, long ago, found carved on stone and baked in clay; from early manuscripts; from the beginning of printing; and since then to our present digital era.

I've selected fifty-two poems from the award-winning illustrated collection called *Something Beginning with P: New Poems from Irish Poets,* which I commissioned with young readers in mind. Poets responded enthusiastically, some telling me they had written their poems as 'gifts' for today's young readers. Extraordinary gifts these are too. I've managed to accommodate half of these poems in this edition (hopefully the other half will appear in a future edition). Many of the gorgeous illustrations from that original collection are here too. Plus one new poem, 'The Supermarket Maw' – here because I'm the editor! And I hate shopping.

Pictures and words, words and pictures: how we understand our world and planet. Enjoy these poems; maybe learn one (or, two) by heart – just for yourself, to say aloud, to whisper or to sing. My wish is that this book will open up for you ways of seeing the world around you and the world within; ways of thinking and imagining; and who knows, ways of writing too, even of writing poems …

Seamus Cashman, Editor

Words Are Such Silly Things

(A playpoem, to be read aloud by four players)
Brendan Kennelly

'O.K., you three guys, let's play the game. What do I spy with my little eye? I spy with my little eye something beginning with — f.

Come on you guys, start guessing.'

'Is it a flower?'
'No!'
'Is it a feather?'
'No!'
'Is it a face?'
'No!' 'Is it a foot?'
'No!'
'Is it a fish?'
'No!'
'Is it a first cousin?'
'No!'
'Is it a frog?'
'No!'
'Is it a frown?'
'No!' 'Is it the future?'
'No!'
'O I give up!'
'And I give up!'
'And I give up!'

[three voices] 'So tell us what it is?'
'O.K. guys, I'll tell you.

It's a fone.'

8

'A phone! But phone

doesn't begin with f.
Phone begins with p-h.
Phone is P-H-O-N-E.

Don't you know that?'

'No, don't be silly!

If **feather** begins with f
And **face** begins with f
And **foot** begins with f
And fish begins with f
And frog begins with f

Then fone must begin with f.'
'No, phone begins with p-h.'

'Why?'

'I don't know
p-h sounds like f in phone.'

'O silly silly silly
words are such silly things —'
'and words are such beautiful things,
        silly and beautiful
                like Mommy's curly head
        when she tries to persuade me
                to go to bed.'

'What about not and knot?'

'And bread and bred?'
'Or lie and lie?'
'And tide and tied?'
'Or down and Down?'
'Or Clare and Clair?'
'Or hair and hare and Molly O'Hare!'

'O stop it, you guys! Let's play again:
Let me see now. O yes.
I spy with my little eye
Something beginning with — O.'

[*three voices*]
'O no, please! No, please! No! No! No!'

(P.S. And what does my granny love to bake?
A tasty inimitable sin-again cake!)

9

Dancing on the Table

Margot Bosonnet

We've got a table
big and square;
we dance on the table
when Mammy's not there.

We've got a table
sturdy and stout;
we dance on the table
when Mammy is out.

We've got a table
and it's able
to be a stage or a mountain top
and underneath is a cave or shop
or the vilest hold of a sailing sloop
where prisoners are chained to the legs by loops.
It's a nomad's tent in the Gobi desert,
it's a snow dugout on the slopes of Everest
in the wildest storm that tries to sweep
us to our deaths,
it's a pothole deep.
It's a caravan trading merchandise,
it's a pond for skating, thick with ice.

We've got a table chipped in patches,
we've got a table with lots of scratches
but it feels so silky when our feet are bare
that we dance on the table and *we* don't care!

We dance on the table
and we clamour and shout;
we dance on the table
till we're all danced out …

Turns

Siobhan Campbell

Back and forth, over and back,
don't you land on the concrete crack.
That's the line between here and never,
skip on it and you won't go to heaven.

In and out, out and in,
how many times can you vote to win?
Fuss them down to town by train,
then back home to vote again.

Over and back, up and over,
how many leaves in a four-leafed clover?
One two three four,
no, you're wrong, it has one more,
the secret drill curled in the stem
that leaves the clover furl its whim.

Over and back, take up my slack,
one of us has to go to the back.
Gently mind or it skims a whip,
watch the line, jump or trip.
Hold it straight or lose the tack.
Ah, you've slipped the concrete crack.

The run is broke.
The turn is took.
The rope is down
and here's the dark.

Txt U L8r

Aislinn O'Loughlin

D gr8 ting bout txt msg cnvrs8ns
s dat u cn uz dese abrvi8ns.
U stp splln wrds d wy dat u auta
& drp sum vwls 2, f dat mks d wrd shrta.

Bt wot f ur so bz b/ng dat clvr
u 4gt hw 2 spll nrml wrds al2gdr?
Coz wit all d ltrs & stf dat wre luzn
dnt u tink rdng dis pom wz cnfuzn?

The Recipe for Happiness

Grace Wells

The recipe for happiness in our house
is to take a cup of flour,
add milk, two eggs, a pinch of salt,
and whisk for half an hour.

Then take the creamy mixture
to the steaming frying pan,
ladle little circles in,
as many as you can.

Watch them all turn gold and brown,
then sit down to eat,
sugar and lemon on one side,
pour maple syrup to complete.

'What are we doing yesterday, Granda?'

a nonsense rime
Máire Mhac an tSaoi

'Inis scéal dom, a Dheaideó.'

'Scéal, scéal,
eireaball ar an éan,
láir bhacach bhúi,
searrach ó sí,
Liam 's a mhac,
liaithe ar leac,
mada rua caorach,
    Ó fada ream!
    Ó fada ream!
    Ó fada ream!
Mada rua caorach,
    Ó fada ream!'

'Cad a dhéanfam inné, a Dheaideo?'
'Fé mar a dheineamar amáireach, a mhaicín.'

Old Witch, Young Witch

Mary O'Donnell

The witch up the road is busily cooking,
stirring the cauldron when no-one is looking.

The thick broth is bubbling with frogs' legs and bats,
and glistening, I think, with the tail-ends of rats.

Our neighbour's not ugly, with warts on her nose,
her smile is so sweet, you'd never suppose

that this is a witch, the vilest one ever.
The thing is, you see, she's awfully clever.

She drives to the school gates every day,
with kids of her own who never would say

that their Ma is a tyrant whose tricks are so vast,
(their mouths buttoned shut by some spell she has cast).

She has charmed even them (not to mention the cat),
to stick by her side and not say what she's at!

She offers some kids sweets of poisonous weeds,
that change in our bellies to hard little beads.

She gives jolly parties, pretends to be nice,
but cross her just once and your head's full of lice.

She knows that I know what she's at in the dark,
out on a broomstick, seeking her mark,

hovering close where the bonfires light,
hunting low over fields for children at night.

But now that I'm growing I've spells of my own,
I know how to stop her by holding two bones

from last Sunday's beef dinner, up to the moon
where I cross them and murmur the words of my rune.

This is the season young witches are growing,
learning the trade without OLD witches knowing!

Word Game

Philip Casey

What am I to the s*ky*? say I.

What are you to the *shoe*? say you

What is he to the flea? says he.

What is she to the Tree? says she.

Hoppy New Year:

a one-legged nursery rhyme

Thomas Kinsella

Winter stiff with frosts and freezes.
Spring renews with warming breezes.
Easter sinks us to our kneeses,
Grateful for the griefs of Jesus.
Summer – bright with birds and beeses.
Autumn – leaves forsake the treeses.
Winter, damp with foul diseases,
Rounds in dark: the season seizes.

What are we to the Sea? say we.

What are you to the zoo? say you.

What are they to the play? say they.

The Great Blue Whale

Kerry Hardie

Nobody knows
where he goes
nor what he does in the deeps,

nor why he sings,
like a bird without wings,
nor where he eats and sleeps.

The blue whale roves
through watery groves,
his heart is the size of a car,

his tongue, on the scale,
makes zoologists pale –
it's as heavy as elephants are.

A blue whale's vein
without stress or strain
could be swum down by you or me.

He's the biggest feature
that ever did creature
the sky, the land or the sea.

Sruthán sa tSeapáin
Nuala Ní Dhomhnaill

Thíos in íochtar an uisce
snámhann na héisc 'ayu'
go gasta
ar an grinneall.

'Ayu, ayu' a bhéicimíd
go sásta
nuair a chímíd iad.

'Ayu, ayu' a smeachaimíd
go blasta
nuair a ithimíd iad.

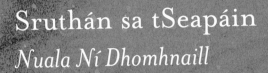

Belly Buttons
Gabriel Fitzmaurice

An 'inny' or an 'outie' — in like Dingle harbour

a belly button goes

or out like the Pope's Nose.

The Love Song of Harry Hippo
Larry O'Loughlin

Harry Hippo fell in love one Sunday afternoon and sang his girlfriend love songs beneath the jungle moon.

'Oh, marry me,' sang Harry, 'and I'll cover you in kisses and be so proud when you become my hippopotamissus.'

20

Sa Bhaile
Una Leavy

Níl aon tinteán
mar do thinteán féin.

Croch suas do chóta,
bain díot do bhróga,
faigh cupán tae agus
suigh cois na tine.

Cuirtíní dúnta,
seanchlog ag bualadh,
gaoth ins an simléar
ag cogar sa chiúnas.

An cat is an madra
'na gcodladh araon.
Níl aon tinteán
mar do thinteán féin.

An 'inny' or an 'outie —'
what kind of one have you?

I wish I had an 'inny' 'cos mine sticks out. Boo hoo!

Cold Day, Hot Day

Joan McBreen

On a cold day
three sparrows
sit together
on the telephone wire,
heads close
to their chests.

On a hot day
three fishes
play —
oh, the fun they have
in the cool caves
beneath the sea.

Three caterpillars
crawling on the wall
take fright
when a voice
says, 'that's tickly!'

Líadan

a poet of the seventh century
Susan Connolly

Five main roads converge at Tara,
monks live on tiny islands,
Newgrange lies tumbledown.

Líadan and Cuirithir hear
the lulling song of the forest,
the roar of a flame-red sea.

Poisoned

John Ennis

All the late sunlit afternoon he lay, my brothers' collie
by the garden hedge, but out the south-facing riverfield side
his white teeth parted in little ivories for his tongue.
Glossy bluebottles circled his open almond eyes.

It must have been late August or so for the pippins
up in the old tall trees ripened red and unseen
the appled side of the hedge where the bitter crab grew.
His bushy tail was rigid and his thin legs were too.

Corn was on the noisy mind of everyone, it seems,
the tall barley bearding you like an older brother, then
oats, wheat as well in the golden sun. After supper, they'd bury him
sorrowing, one to the other, for he never bothered sheep.

And I who loved to reach up my two arms
to meet round his ruff neck, rub the slender nose that tapered
or touch the black-tipped ears that looked forward,
hurried on by in the hot sun for his flies lit on me
and I was so afraid in my heart of the dead.

My Family, When I'm Angry

Jo Slade

My silly sister squabble sings,
'If I were a blackbird I'd whistle and sing …'

If I were a blackbird I'd be out of here.
I'd be the only bird on the wing —
a lone migrator to an unknown land
not mapped, never seen, an island for
the dropped in and leaving soon.
No gods, saints, mystics, angels,
wise old crabs, archetypes, visionaries,
no next of kin, kind old gran, friend of the family.
No one I know or have ever seen.

Nope, I'll jump ship, drown
I just won't hang around.
I won't 'Polly put the kettle on'.
I'll hide — be a wheel in the garden
an oil tank overgrown with leaves,
I'll tell the cops I live with thieves.

Higgledy, piggledy, powder and gun
hide in the dustbin or they'll kill you for fun.

24

Síofra Sí
Celia de Fréine

Bíonn Síofra Sí
sióg na bhfiacla
ag obair léi
gach uile oíche

ag eitilt go tapaidh
ó theach go teach
ag bailiú fiacla
go cúramach

ag lóisteáil airgid
faoi bhun piliúr
ag bronnadh sonais
gach uile uair

ag brostú abhaile
le breacadh an lae
ag súil go mór
lena cupán tae.

Hallowe'en
Michael Longley

It is Hallowe'en. Turnip head
Will soon be given his face,
A slit, two triangles, a hole.
His brains litter the table top.
A candle stub will be his soul.

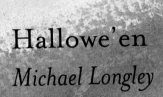

Robot Kid

Patrick Chapman

Imagine being built with bolts
and powered by a million volts.
You'd have to wear a glove to shake
the hands of other kids — or make

them disappear in puffs of smoke!
And then you'd have to play and joke
with different children every week
because your friends were always — Eek! —

exploding, until one smart kid
unplugged you from the power grid.
And then you'd sleep for evermore,
your only sound, a robot snore.

So thank your lucky, lucky stars
and some small planets, that you are
a kid of flesh and blood — and not
a super-voltage kid robot.

Santa's Poem

Sean Clarkin

The dogs in the streets were surprised, not impressed,
by this apparition funnily dressed.

The children standing half-in the hall
knew the night that I would call.

I rang my bell and announced the news:
(Was I really in Santa's shoes!)

'Everybody has his burden to bear,'
the butcher laughed as I passed his door.

I was Town Crier from far away.
Message and Messenger for one day.

Lifting his cap to reveal his hair
Dunphy the Postman crossed the floor.

By Michael Street I was growing red.
'SANTA'S IN TOWN' the poster said.

I was tickly and sweaty and awfully sore
(the big boots) when I reached the store.

They laughed or loved me for many an hour
those children who now are fewer and fewer.

Shane the Shaman

Máighréad Medbh

Who's a rabbit, who's a bear?
Who's a fox and who's a hare?
Who's a tree and who's an eagle on the wing?
Who's a human, who's a cow?
Who's a snake and who's an owl?
Who's a crow and who's an orca who can sing?

Shane the Shaman takes the beating of the earth
to be inside him and his heart begins a drumming
to the rhythm of its humming,
and its whirring and its buzzing
and its chewing and its mooing
and the turning and the churning
and the colours cool and burning,
and the infinite returning
of the sun at every morning …
and the night with all its crooning
and its moody deep blue mooning
and the stars that blaze and shatter
in the infinite dark matter.

He's gone flying, he's gone scrying,
like a seagull wild and crying,
on the waves for silver fishes,
who have eyes that grant you wishes.
If you saw him now you'd wonder
why his body's in a stupor
and he doesn't feel you touch him,
know you're near or hear you talking.

He's gone walking in his mind
to where the spirits and their kind
are in a flurry, and they scurry
when they see his soul is coming.

He will wander in the dark until
a sign appears so stark
that he can't miss it: it's a letter
with a charm to make us better.
He's a postman from the darkness,
where we all have second cousins.
For every one we see here,
there's another, doppelganger,
maybe angels, maybe spirits,
maybe particles of matter.

That's what Shane believes he knows,
like the holy men of old,
when the animals and trees
gave their spirits to the breeze.

Back he's coming to the drumming
and the quiet sound of humming,
to his fingers and his toes,
legs and shoulders, mouth and nose;
to his body's wonder-vessel,
where his mind is in control.
Eyes are opened, here's the message –
maybe healing for your soul.

You can't talk to Shane the Shaman
like you would to other children.
He's been places you can't dream of,
wild and lonely, dark and cold.
He's been off to see great wonders —
moving mountains, talking clouds;
he's met monsters, walked on rivers,
jumped a chasm, led a crowd.
But he's just as good a friend,
plays a game and kicks a ball,
and you might just need his healing
in the summer when you fall.

Who's a rabbit, who's a bear?
Who's a fox and who's a hare?
Who's a tree and who's an eagle on the wing?
Who's a human, who's a cow?
Who's a snake and who's an owl?
Who's a crow and who's an orca who can sing?

Do you know what the sea is able to do?

Pat Ingoldsby

Do you know what the sea is able to do?
For all of her millions and billions and trillions of tons,
her rocks and her wrecks, her seaweed and stones,
her mermaids and serpents, mysterious bones,
her tempests to test you, fish that can fly,
pinkeens that are gone in the wink of an eye,
whirlpools to suck you as if you're a sweet,
sharks who would shred you like yesterday's wheat,

do you *know* what the sea is able to do?

She is able to lie perfectly still
without uttering a sound,
quiet as a feather adrift on the ground.

I find that almost impossible to do.
What do you think? ... Me too!

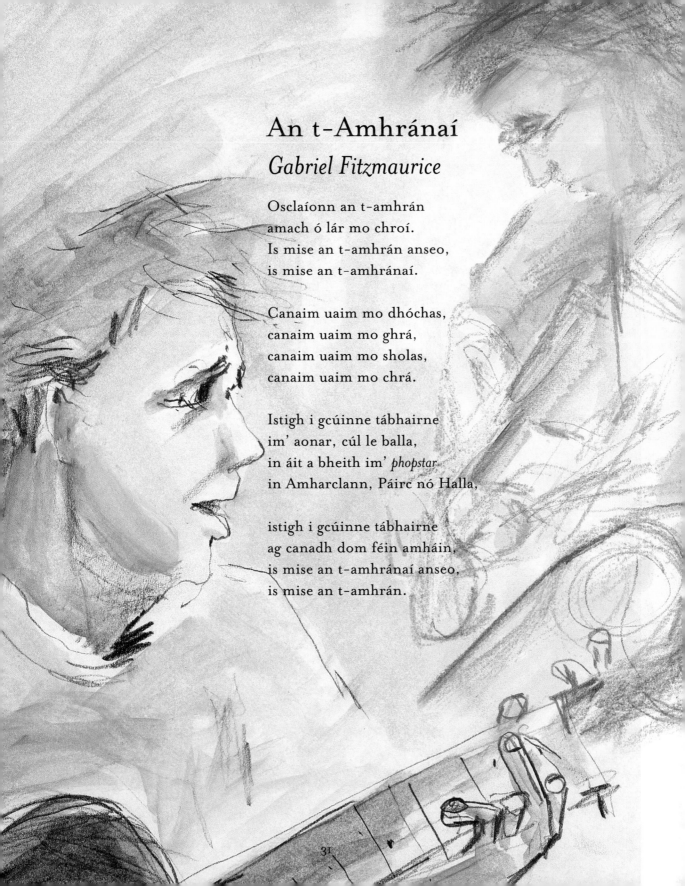

An t-Amhránaí

Gabriel Fitzmaurice

Osclaíonn an t-amhrán
amach ó lár mo chroí.
Is mise an t-amhrán anseo,
is mise an t-amhránaí.

Canaim uaim mo dhóchas,
canaim uaim mo ghrá,
canaim uaim mo sholas,
canaim uaim mo chrá.

Istigh i gcúinne tábhairne
im' aonar, cúl le balla,
in áit a bheith im' *phopstar*
in Amharclann, Páirc nó Halla,

istigh i gcúinne tábhairne
ag canadh dom féin amháin,
is mise an t-amhránaí anseo,
is mise an t-amhrán.

The North Pole
Frank McGuinness

The ice built that house.
Frozen windows allowed in
what light they could.
Two bedrooms
measuring day by darkness
touched cold and turned
the heart to red
sleet and snow.
Men cried and
women listened.
Women cried and
turned to stone.

In the bare garden
red children played
games of fast and loose,
lucky sods to leave
that path of hardened,
headstrong ground
where nothing grew but
sorest, sourest rock.
Women cried and
men listened.
Men cried and
turned to stone.

Winter froze forever
the kitchen table,
the scullery,
the living room.
Floors turned into
deadly weapons
sharp as silver forks,
red as meat on knives.
Children cried and
learned to listen,
children cried and
turned to stone.

Oidhreacht

Áine Ní Ghlinn

Tusa a chabhraigh liom
na huibheacha a chomhaireamh
sa nead spideoige a bhí folaithe
ag an eidhneán ag bun an ghairdín.

Tusa a bhain an leabhar mór anuas ón seilf
a chuaigh tríd leathanach ar leathanach
nó go bhfacamar
uibheacha ár spideoige.

Tusa a rinne roicéad liom
as cathaoir chistine
is a bhí mar chomhphíolóta agam
ar ár gcéad thuras go Mars.

Tusa a chaith na laethanta fada liom
ag faire ar na damháin alla is na péisteanna
a shiúil abhaile liom faoi ualach duilleogach
ár bpócaí ag cur thar maoil le hiontaisí na coille.

Tusa an té a raibh an t-am agat
is a roinn an t-am sin liomsa.
Anois agus tearmann do láimhe móiré imithe uaim
beidh oidhreacht do chuid ama agam go deo.

The Supermarket Maw

Seamus Cashman

Once out
I take the nearest escalator to the next floor.
I don't know why for I have no business there:
no ceiling to paint, nor jewellery to buy.
Back-tracking from the post-office,
a whisper in my brain says
'milk, bread and parsnips'
as I pass a supermarket maw.

The threshold crossing splashes me in-colour
streams that course through my gullet
to pool as sillion – clumps of clay
in an empty stomach. I stop to get out
my glasses, polish lenses for clarity.

I take stock, already surrounded
by brash countertops of raw meat,
iced fish, rack-fulls of root veg and crinkly
lettuce heads. The boldly branded stands
of stuffed bread-wrappers screech where they hawk
under a surgical flight of white bulbs.
To my right are the streets of New York
crowded with trolley people. My feet lock.

10.30 of a Wednesday morning
and this flooded byway drenched
under an adhesive glare.
Pocketing my glasses I re-tune,
swivel, hurry out to an escalator
—that slows me—
towards the nearest exit.

Medley for Morin Khur

Paul Muldoon

The sound box is made of a horse's head.
The resonator is horse skin.
The strings and bow are of horsehair.

I

The Morin Khur is the thoroughbred
of Mongolian violins.
Its call is the call of the stallion to the mare.

II

A call which may no more be gainsaid
than that of jinn to jinn
through jasmine-weighted air.

IV

A call that may no more be gainsaid
than that of blood kin to kin
through a body-strewn central square.

V

A square in which they'll heap the horse heads
by the heaps of horse skin
and the heaps of horsehair.

Skinhead

Mark Granier

My brother had so many hard knocks
he should have stayed in bed.
Instead,
he bought a brand-new pair of *Docs*
and shaved his head.

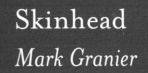

Street Dancer

Gabriel Rosenstock

There once was a boy who danced on the street,
danced with his arms, danced with his feet.
He danced all day from the sun's first light –
danced with stars in the purple night.
'Nothing to lose!' he cried, 'Nothing to lose!
nothing at all but the soles on my shoes!'
And people would stop and stare a while
shaking their heads with a little smile …
Sometimes he'd wriggle and sometimes he'd shake –
sometimes he even danced like a snake.
At times he was wild, at times he was tame –
no two dances were ever the same.
He had names for his dances: Falling Snow
was the name of a dance that was terribly slow.
He made up others as he went along:
Polish Goose and Tibetan Gong.
Sometimes he'd chant or sometimes he'd hum –
mostly he just preferred to be stumm.
Was he born to dance? Nobody knows …
but when he was born he wriggled his toes.
He was dancing as soon as he learned to walk
dancing before he was able to talk.
'Hello, I see you're dancing too!'
he once exclaimed to a shy bamboo.

One day he met a holy man
who said, 'Things dance as best they can!
Everything – look! Even that table!
No, nothing is solid, nothing is stable!'
And the boy understood that dancing was good,
everything dances as everything should.
'Well, I'll dance the blue sky!' the little boy said,
'I'll dance the green sea and the flat ocean bed,

I'll dance for the young, dance for the old,
dance in the heat, dance in the cold.
I'll dance every colour, dance every sound,
dance in the air, dance on the ground.
I'll dance you a river! Dance you a lake,
the falling leaves and the crooked rake.
Dance you the whales that roam the sea,
dance you Time and Eternity.
The sickle moon, the planet Mars,
the thousands and thousands and millions of stars!

Yes, I will become the dance,' said he,
'I am the dance, the dance is me!'

Van Gogh's Yellow Chair

Mark Roper

I would love to sit
in the yellow chair
in the painting,

when a shadow lies
like a shy animal
in a corner

and the day's air
is like water in which
small noises swim.

I would light my pipe
and watch
the blue smoke rise,

I would sit there
safe from harm,
safe from all surprise.

Beyond the frame
on every side
the outside world

would open wide,
but I'd have crossed
the great divide.

Nothing could touch me
if I sat there.
I would live forever

so long as I never
rose from
that yellow chair.

Me in a Tree

Julie O'Callaghan

Unfortunately, it wasn't
a luxury tree house
with hot and cold running cocoa
or with a robin

bringing me breakfast in bed.
A squirrel didn't toss acorns
at me when I needed to wake up.
No – that wasn't how it was.

I hid high up in the leaves.
So many thoughts were floating,
I speared them on to twigs
to see them twinkle in the sun.

But now I realise
I named this poem the wrong thing.
It's not me in a tree.
It's the tree in me.

Ceist

Rody Gorman

Sea, ceist agam ort,
a chéirseach:
nuair a chasann tú an fonn sin
ar maidin go luath,
an bhfuil tú ag labhairt leat díreach
mar ba dhual do do leithéid a riamh
nó ag tabhairt le taispeáint
d'aon oghaim dom féin?

An Bhóín Dé

Tom Mac Intyre

Thaispeáin tú thú féin –
leigheas is saineolaí –
i lár an leathanaigh bháin.

D'fhagas im ghairdín thú
is, támáilteach ó dhúchas,
rinneas dearmad ort, a stór,

go dtí gur stopais mo shúil
aréir: tusa ar ais, beo
beathach, i bhfréamhacha taibhrimh
– lasair, bé choille, is seoid.

The Heron
Rita Kelly

In an air full of river-spray
the heron stands at weir-edge.
Absolutely still,
deadly still,
frozen still.

A small wind ruffles
a few neck feathers;
they are pure white.

His long legs look like twigs.
Her long legs look like twigs.
So thin,
how can they carry this big grey-blue body?

When she sits on her nest
her legs stick out, hang
down, untidy.
It is an untidy kind of nest.
A big clump of twigs
picked and gleaned,
gathered, pushed and shoved
into some form of shape.

But it is still a clump
low enough in the willow tree.

I love that heron,
so often alone,
by the weir,
who climbs up the air
with languid wing
when I come within sight of him.

Oh the tedium of people walking by
just when she has stared that fish to death.
A second before snatching it out of the water
with killer precision.

Once, just once,
I saw him and her together –
of course I never know which of them
stands on the weir –
there were two herons
perched
as if in a Chinese print,
with sweep of tail, and ever-watching eye,
on the bare, mossed, willow tree.
And then there came two more.
Another pair came too and two more as well
all finding spaces for themselves
beneath the clumpy nest.

It was indeed a mighty heron fest.

Neighbourhood Watch

Anne Le Marquand Hartigan

I know your dog is old and weary
for him his days grow slow and dreary
his legs are stiff, he stops and staggers

his tail now only limply waggers
his eyes, like mine have deepening baggers
but still he does his job for you – deposits

large and juicy poos.

Please, dear Neighbour, do me one favour
it is a point I fain would labour
those doggy shits I do not savour –

dear Neighbour do you care one bit
where your hound-dog does his shit?
Please look beside my garden railings

brown deposits, spied through pailings
squashy, dried or decomposing
other doggies sometimes nosing –

these relics – I do not enjoy. So
with a shovel please deploy
them to some other place –

I dare you sir to show your face
why should I have this disgrace-
full mess around my place?

How dare you, sir, let him totter
you can't care one little jotter
that he poos inside my gate

where my poor foot, when I come late
on doggie excrement does skate –
would you like it on your plate

for breakfast?

Neighbour, I have had enough,
things are getting pretty tough
and so am I.

Halt, dear Neighbour, vengeance rises
I am thinking sweet surprises
dressed in horrid nasty guises

if you do not change your ways.

You will cry and howl for mercy
as my rage comes down to curse ye
my anger getting worse and worsie,

I'm heaping up a tidy pile
getting deeper all the while
I am savouring my bile –

accept this now – my final hit
as in your letter box I fit
about a ton of doggy shit.

The Sock Gatherer

Thomas McCarthy

Patient as any four-legged companion, Elvis, our dog
endures the constant traffic of our human house:
day-long he tolerates the noise of X-Box
and PlayStation 2, expletives that follow
a wrong choice of weapon, accidental thumps on the head
that fall from on high in the form of cushions and shoes;
and forgetfulness, our unforgivable human trait —
oh dear! A door closes upon him in heavy rain
and he, unsung hero, as heroic as Tom Crean
retains his composure while turning into a downpipe.
As for meals forgotten, and the sight of his water-bowl
on the wrong side of a locked gate in mid-August,
I don't dare to mention them, his tolerance being saintly.

Except at night. For at night he extracts a small tribute
from our human kingdom. At night he is a tax-gatherer,
moving from room to room while we are still disconnected
from machines, while we are parallel with him —
Neil's best Nike socks, Kate's multi-coloured leggings,
Cathy's best cottons, my own mouldy socks for boots,
one by one (not pair by pair) he drags them to his basket.
There they are hoarded as an honorarium for dogs,
a reward for the faithful; a pillow for his damp nose.

Head Lice

Terry McDonagh

I've had head lice
twice …   scratch … scratch.

Nearly went bananas, I did.
Worse than bad breath, it was.
Good mates defect to
enemy gangs, take the lice
with them and keep on

                    scratching.

My things were put
in the freezer
to frostbite the life
out of the geezers …   scratch.

I cried for my teddy
in his cold, cold cot …   scratch.

A teacher got lice four times.
The kids went wild and cheered.
The teacher went home … scratch.

They get into hair
and into clothes
and onto pillows
and onto car seats
and onto toys
and onto teddies
and onto friends.

They get around …   scratch.

One kid took
a photo of a louse
and enlarged it.
It looked like a mouse.
A small girl fainted.
Oh, my God!   Scratch.

Some say super lice
that can't be killed
are on the way.

Don't let this happen,

please …   scratch.

My friend said
her whole class
had head lice
at her last school
and they scratched
    and scratched
    and scratched

scratch   scratch   scratch   scratch
scratch   scratch

scratch

crat

scratch

Pearl and the Rhymes

Justin Quinn

There was a bunch of rhymes
out looking for a girl
to put her in a poem.
Along came one called Pearl.

The first rhyme said to her:

'You're such a dirty pup.
Come here, I'll clean you up
and scrape you with a comb
and put you in our poem.'

Pearl nearly ran away …

But the next rhyme said to her:

'You don't look well to me.
I'll feed you broccoli
and carrots from our home.
You'll be fit for our poem.'

Pearl nearly ran away …

But the next rhyme said to her:

'Your clothes are such a mess!
Put on this nice pink dress
with frilly bits like foam.
You'll look cute in our poem.'

Pearl nearly ran away …

But the last rhyme said to her:

'No scraping with a comb.
No carrots from our home.
No frilly bits like foam.
For really it's your poem
where you can come and play
just as you are and stay
an hour or for a day.
Come on, what do you say?'

Pearl didn't run away.

A Keen for the Coins

Seamus Heaney

O henny penny! O horsed half-crown!
O florin salmon! O sixpence hound!
O woodcock! Piglets! Hare and bull!
O mint of field and flood, farewell!
Be Ireland's lost ark, gone to ground,
And where the rainbow ends, be found.

Mornsong
Dennis O'Driscoll

Rise in the morning,
face the unknown.
Iron your skin
and polish your bone.

Eat up your breakfast
of pie in the sky.
Your thoughts are the best
that pennies can buy.

Clouds are like dripping
stuck to a bowl.
Rain is a mare
giving birth to a foal.

It's time you left home
for the front of the class.
The wider the mark,
the greater the gas.

Your school is a lab
where test tubes play pranks.
Your class is a form
where you fill in your blanks.

Pack a lunch of smoked apples
or cornflakes and fries.
Splash out on fresh rainshine,
yawn open your eyes.

House Proud

Frank Ormsby

You'll like our porch.
To put you at your ease
our Laughing Buddha
chimes on every breeze.

Our lantern porchlight
joys in shadow-play.
Its daylight sensor
keeps the dark at bay.

Inside our walls are panelled.
The stained glass
on the landing
exudes a certain gravitas.

Christmas trees and luggage
take a year
out in our attic.
Dust loves to settle here.

On winter days
our heated kitchen floor
would tempt you to kick
your shoes off at the door.

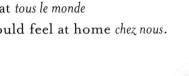

Our conservatory hosts the sun.
Here even showers
are therapeutic.
At night the moon is ours.

Our north-facing garden
is the place to go
for snow and blackbirds —
in case you didn't know!

Nothing pretentious. We think
you'll share our view
that *tous le monde*
would feel at home *chez nous*.

Miracle Boy

Catherine Phil MacCarthy

You learn tricks
on a new BMX,
wheelies
and bunny hops,

gain speed and loop
long back a hoop
against azure
birthday skies.

The weather pitch
half-laid is rich
as a cinder path,
terrain to pull

bars into the air
as if it were
your own element
and flight second nature.

You've taught me to see
you defy gravity,
speak the lingo
for where would life be

without rotations,
funky chickens,
infinity rolls?
Despite fear

of losing control,
falls and wipe-outs,
as you clear a ramp
or a half-pipe,

your passion sparks
taking risks,
wheels, wings
riding thermals

in an open sky,
like that boy
who ran free
of the labyrinth

and flew so high:
dare I pry —
of these cheats
of mortality,

this hunger
for eternity
amid all the buzz —
if you know Icarus?

Tree
Katie Donovan

I am out in the wind
and standing firm.

It's not like
being taken in
and showered
in silver.

Not like
being dressed in light,
my scent
lifting the room.

This is where
I don't have
to cut off
my roots.

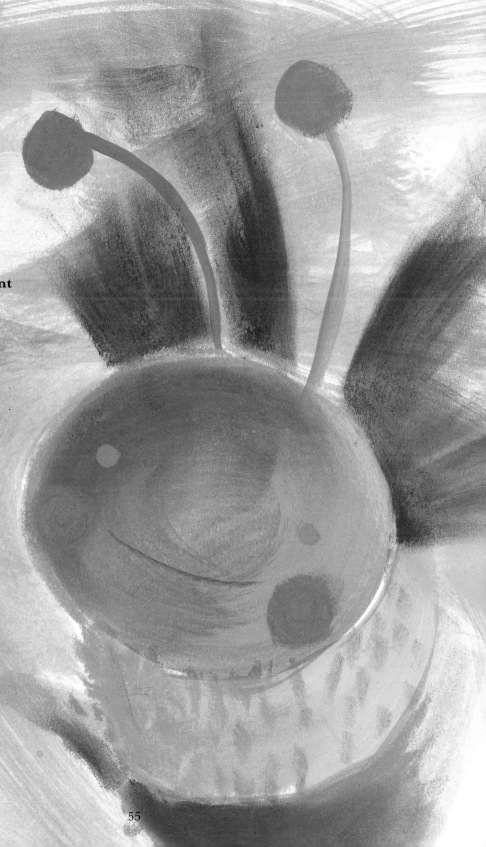

Bee-chasing
Nessa O'Mahony

You stalk
eying montbretia flames
levelling ferns …

now stock-still
tracking a bee's flight,
waiting for the exact point
in its trajectory
to pounce,

the learned grace
of an aerial acrobat
claws
arching
as you complete
a perfect somersault …

and miss once more.

Outside
a car brakes;
ears flatten
as you arrow back
to safety.

Bully
Enda Wyley

You are a sharp pencil
in my side during every class,
a robber of all the homework I do,
a smiling, sweet face to the teacher
but a hissing, green-eyed demon to me.

You are cruel glass in the playground,
a towering wall that blocks my way home.
You push, kick, bruise, taunt, sneer, laugh
at me – there is nowhere you won't find me.
My nights and mornings have your cruel stare.

But there'll come a time when you'll fall down,
when you'll cry out, when you'll be left alone.
Then who will help you up, dry your eyes, brush
dust from your knees, gently wash your cuts clean?
Who will take your hand and walk home with you?

TXT—UR

Paula Meehan

Wots d crak? Its Mick frm d plex. Keiths m8.
In d park. Wanna stall it? Bring a cr8!

N me way. Is dat uzer fire B-side d g8?

N.e chance of hukn-up again? Last-nite woz gr8!

STOP THIS OBSCENITY AT ONCE. KATE'S

MAM HERE. I'LL CALL THE GUARDS. YOU REPROBATE!

U prik, im groundid. D lox r changed! Just u w8
til me Da gets iz handz n u! He'l b8

lumps outta u!
                          Lets start again. A cleen sl8.
Dnt wrk ureself up n2 such a st8!

Last of me cred! Rekn me hed! 2 much n me pl8.
Dnt even no if dis is luv r if dis is h8!

Dats cool chix, but dnt leev it 2 l8.
Deyre Q-ing up 4 me all over dis est8!!

I'm Not Stupid

Moyra Donaldson

Shouting rises
above the sound of the TV,
up through the ceiling, seeping
between the floorboards of my room
until I put my headphones on and tune it out,
get homework done, despite my parents arguing.

Tomorrow they'll
pretend it's all ok, tell me
there's nothing to worry about,
as if I'm just a kid and don't know
what's happening, mum's eyes all red from crying,
dad not talking and drinking too much and maybe leaving.

Do they think I'm stupid? That I don't know what's going on?

Leaving for a Nursing Home

Pádraig J Daly

She reaches a thin hand
to clutch at mine:
She is frail and frightened.

She must leave all that years
have made familiar
and go where she will lie at night

listening to the moans of strangers.
No more dusting jugs and photographs,
setting out cups,

filling at evening her hot water jar,
putting the door on double lock,
climbing the short stairs to her bedroom.

If a clock ticks, it will not be hers.
If a phone rings in the night,
it will be for some other.

Amen Woman

Noel Monahan

She was in love with colours,
streaks in her hair,
peacock feathers grew in her hat.
November winds danced on her summer dress
and she always said: *Amen, Amen*.

She pushed a wheelbarrow full of gadgets
through the streets,
shouting: lamp shades – clothes pegs – sun glasses –
nibs for pens – bottles for rheumatism;
and finally she would say: *Amen, Amen*.

She could call at any time
of day or night, front door, back door.
The cat kept a nervous eye on her,
the dog barked furiously
and she calmed him with her *Amen, Amen*.

She told us all the news,
who was getting married – what happened to Eileen
and more if you listened –
about Ukulele Joe and his midnight parties
and then she'd say, *Amen, Amen*, and trundle away.

She got lost somewhere
disappeared in the fog –
someone said she went to a brother in America,
others say she was old enough to die,
grew wings and flew to heaven, *Amen, Amen*.

Blue Willow
Mary O'Malley

By the moongate in Denis's garden
there's a pond. Shoals of tangerine fishes
blow bubbly kisses. A young pearl fisher
dives in to pick them. They turn to moon opals
a necklace of wishes for his princess.

Over there under the monkey-puzzle tree
there's a unicorn, sitting pretty
exactly like the famous tapestry in France
he has his silly eye on you but don't worry
he's a bit of a prancy dancer.

Now your tiger with his stripes on fire is rippling
through the moongate in Denis's garden.
Cool cool fiery cat, close your eyes and fancy that
    by the silvery zip-zapping scissory rip-rapping
      only pretending-to-sleep napping sea.

In the Desert

Eiléan Ní Chuilleanáin

Almost day, looking down
from my high tower in the desert:
the sandstorm blows up
cuts my tower in half:
a crooked scarf of sand
as high as the window
that looks towards the mountains.
I cover my eyes
with my red scarf that slants
wrapping my body
and when it is over
I look towards the desert
and I see him again
in the daybreak light
still walking nearer —
he must be half-blinded.

In the desert walking
I see them by the shining,
reflection of dawn light,
something bright sewn in the cloth
worn on the head
masking the face.
I see them glinting.

He is sand brown,
his clothes brown like sand.
Now he is closer,
I see his shadow
as the dawn rises,
a bending shadow
and he approaches the well
in the shade of the palm trees.

Coming to the well he lifts
its wooden covering. Night
and coolness are still down there.
The snakes lie in the well, males
and females coiled together, wet.
Before he dips his cup to drink
he salutes them saying, happy
snakes, like the poor people,
who have only the comfort men
and women find in each other.
Let me fill my cup, let me rest
here in the shadow.

I hear him praying, I see him drink.
He lies down in the shadow.
When will somebody come and release me
from the sand-frayed tower, from the red scarf
that covers me like a flame?

TRANSLATIONS

I am very grateful to Diarmuid Ó Cathasaigh and to individual poets for assistance in preparing (and in some instances for providing) these prose translation guides for non-Irish speaking readers. Any errors in these texts are mine. *Editor.*

[13] Máire Mhac an tSaoi: *What are we doing yesterday, Granda?' a nonsense rime*
'Tell me a story, Granda.' 'A story, a story, a tail on the bird, a lame yellow mare, a foal since she it is. Liam and his son bleached on a stone / a fox minding sheep, O for the ram! O for the ram! O for the ram! a fox minding sheep, O for the ram!' 'What are we doing yesterday, Granda?' 'The same as we did tomorrow, children!'

[19] Nuala Ní Dhomhnaill: *Sruthán sa tSeapáin / A Stream in Japan*
Down at the bottom of the water swims the 'ayu' fish briskly on the river bed. 'Ayu, ayu' we shout happily when we see them. 'Ayu, ayu' we smack our lips tastily when we eat them.

[21] Úna Leavy: *Sa Bhaile / At Home*
There's no fireside like your own fireside. Hang up your coat, take off your shoes, get a cup of tea and sit by the fire. The curtains drawn, the old clock ticking, wind in the chimney whispering in the silence. The cat and the dog both asleep. There is no fireside like your own.

[25] Celia de Fréine: *Síofra Sí / Síofra the Fairy*
Síofra Sí the tooth fairy works every night flying fast from house to house, collecting teeth carefully, lodging money under pillows, bestowing happiness every time, hurrying home at break of day, looking forward to her cup of tea.

[31] Gabriel Fitzmaurice: *An t-Amhránaí / The Singer*
The song opens out from the centre of my heart — I am the song here, I am the singer. I sing my hope, I sing my love, I sing my light, I sing my trouble. In the corner of a pub on my own, back to the wall, instead of being a popstar in Theatre, Park or Hall, in the corner of a pub singing for just myself, I am the singer here, I am the song.

[34] Áine Ní Ghlinn: *Oidhreacht / Legacy*
You were the one who helped me count the eggs in the robin's nest we found hidden in the ivy at the foot of the garden. You were the one who took the book down from the shelf and went through it page by page until we found our robin's eggs. You were the one who helped me make a rocket from a kitchen chair, my co-pilot on our first trip to Mars. You were the one who spent long days with me watching spiders and worms, walking home laden down with leaves, our pockets overflowing with the wonders of the wood. You were the one who had time and who shared that time with me. And although the sanctuary of your big hand is gone the legacy of that time will stay with me forever.

[42] Rody Gorman: *Ceist / A Question*
Yes, a question for you, O thrush [my love]: when you sing forth that tune early in the morning, are you communing [speaking] in the way your sort always do, or focusing your song intentionally on me?

[42] Tom Mac Intyre: *An Bhóín Dé / The Ladybird*
You show yourself — healer and store of wisdom [expert] — in the centre of the white page. I left you in my garden and, timid by nature, I forgot about you, my love, until my eyes closed last night: and there you were, back, alive and well, enframed in bright dreams, nymph of the woods, and jewel.

INDEX OF POETS

The Illustrators

Corrina Askin: 10, 11, 14, 15, 18, 19, 25, 29, 31, 34, 38, 39, 48, 50, 51, 54, 55, 56, 58, 60, 61, 62

Emma Byrne: 7, 8, 9, 16, 17, 20, 21, 35, 47, 57

Alan Clarke: 12, 13, 22, 23, 24, 26, 27, 30, 32, 33, 36, 37, 40, 41, 42, 43, 44, 45, 46, 49, 52, 53, 59